First published in the United States, Great Britain, Canada, Australia, and New Zealand in 2015
by NorthSouth Books, Inc., an imprint of NordSüd Verlag AG, CH-8005 Zürich, Switzerland.

Distributed in the United States by NorthSouth Books, Inc., New York 10016.
Library of Congress Cataloging-in-Publication Data is available.
ISBN: 978-0-7358-4214-4
1 3 5 7 9 • 10 8 6 4 2

Printed in Germany by Grafisches Centrum Cuno GmbH & Co. KG, Calbe, October 2014.

www.northsouth.com

ANKE WAGNER • ANNE-KATHRIN BEHL

HELP,
I DON'T WANT
A BABYSITTER!

North
South

Ollie was very nervous.

Mommy and Daddy were going out tomorrow night. To the movies. So a babysitter was coming to take care of Ollie. And, of course, Stubbs . . .

Stubbs was Ollie's best cuddle buddy, and always had been.

"It'll be exciting," said Mommy and Daddy. "And you get to stay up late."

"We get to stay up late," Ollie announced to Stubbs. "It will be exciting!"

Yippee! Hooray! thought Stubbs.

He loved playing in the golden evening sunlight.

"A babysitter is coming to look after us," explained Ollie.

Stubbs was pale with shock. *What? A babysitter?! There are no babies here!*

"I'm sure the babysitter will be nice," said Ollie.

Stubbs was horrified. *This can't be happening!*

There was no way Stubbs would be able to sleep.

It was true. Later that night, Stubbs tossed and turned. *What would the babysitter be like?*

Stubbs had never seen one.

What if the babysitter wears too much lipstick and too many bows?
What if she only talks about the color pink?

What if she sprays Ollie and Stubbs with stinky perfume?

Just like girls!

Help!

What if the babysitter is
a pumped-up muscleman?

What if he gets Ollie and Stubbs
in a headlock?

Until we pass out.

Help!

What if the babysitter is a strict old aunt who only cooks yucky green vegetables?

What if she makes Ollie and Stubbs eat it all up?

Help!

What if the babysitter is a fussy neat freak?
What if the babysitter forces Ollie and Stubbs to clean their room until it gleams in the golden evening sunlight?

Help!

What if the babysitter is a dozy sleepyhead who falls asleep in front of the TV...

...and doesn't play with Ollie and Stubbs at all?

What if the babysitter is a wicked witch with an evil cackle?

What if she drags Ollie and Stubbs
around by their hair?

Help!

Oh, if we only knew who was coming!
Finally Stubbs fell asleep. He was tired from so much
thinking.

The next evening somebody rang the doorbell.
It was a smiley girl named Ella.
She looks nice, thought Ollie.
She doesn't look anything like a witch, thought Stubbs.

Once Mommy and Daddy left, Ella asked, "Shall we cook
a pirates' feast for supper to make us big and strong?
Swashbucklers' spaghetti with bloodred tomato sauce?"
"Aye, aye!" cried Ollie and Stubbs.
"And afterward a delicious dessert. With extra ice cream!"

"Are you too tired to play hide-and-seek?" asked Ella.

"No way! Not a chance!"

"Whoever gets found has to sing a song in their silliest, squeakiest voice!"

They all laughed until their tummies hurt.

"I don't suppose you have a fort?" asked Ella. "I know a story that can only be read in a fort."

Ollie and Stubbs helped Ella build a cozy fort. Then snuggled up together as she told her tale.

The story was funny and a little bit scary, and left them tingling with excitement.

It was a looong story. Ollie and Stubbs started to feel sooo tired.

They could hardly hold their toothbrushes!

Ella helped them both to bed.

As soon as their heads hit the pillow, they both sank into a sleep as deep as the bottom of the deep blue sea.

When they woke up, they found a note hanging on their bed.
It said:

Dear Ollie and Stubbs,
I had a great evening with you!
Send your parents to the movies again soon.
Then I can come an
another story.
Love,
Ella

Mommy and Daddy, wasn't the movie fun? You should definitely go out more often.

Well, that's what Ollie and Stubbs thought!